The Forbidden Door

Marilee Heyer

VIKING KESTREL

The next warm summer night, when you stare at the stars overhead, search for the smallest one—for on that star in the Valley of the Bao-Bickle tree lived a young girl named Reena, who had never seen the Sun, nor had her parents, nor their parents before them. In fact, they didn't know it existed, for they all lived in a cave beneath the ground. In times past, the cave had been filled with happy, peaceful people. Now only Reena and her parents remained.

Don't feel sorry for them. They loved their cave, for it was truly wondrous, with more rooms than you could count in a year, each one filled with furniture carved in the finest detail, and with shimmering tapestries, all made by Reena's ancestors.

There was one special room they went to every day: the room with the luminous walls. There the trees grew that gave them life, trees that bore fruit year-round and whose leaves could be spun into thread for cloth. Together Reena and her parents tended them with care.

In the evening the three of them would sit around their warm fire and Reena's parents would carve toys for her, anything she could imagine, for she had no other children to play with and they loved her and didn't want her to be lonely.

Of all her toys, Reena's favorite was a puppet theater, with a painted sky and gold stars. Neither Reena nor her parents knew it was the sky. They had just copied the design from one of the many old tapestries.

The evenings were also for story time, the time Reena loved best. Each night she would sit quietly as her parents told different stories of the ancestors who once lived in the now-deserted rooms.

One evening, Reena's mother told a story very different from all the others, an older story, one she herself could barely remember. It was about a place called Outside. As her mother began to speak, Reena's father touched her arm as if to silence her, but she went on. She was telling of the things called *flowers* and *mountains* and *sky*, like Reena's puppet theater sky, but for the first time she mentioned a place where they all became real and alive—Outside.

There was something else new in the story, something that made Reena's eyes glow, as if a spark from the fire had jumped into them. Her mother was telling of a huge red burning orb called the Sun.

"Mother, please can we go to this wonderful place," Reena cried.

Her mother blinked as if waking from a long sleep, and took her daughter into her arms.

"Forgive me, Reena," she whispered. "I should not have told you that story. We can never go to this place. It is only a dream of the old ones. We must never speak of it again. It is forbidden."

Forbidden? Tears filled Reena's eyes, not because of this cold new word, but because her mother's lovely face looked so white and distant. She looked at her father, and he too looked lost and faraway.

Indeed, this oldest of stories, once spoken, had awakened sad memories within her parents of other old stories about ancient loved ones who had mysteriously disappeared.

Reena hugged her mother close and vowed to forget about Outside and the Sun.

She did try very hard to forget, but the more she tried, the more thoughts of Outside crept into her mind. If she succeeded in thinking of other things during the day, then at night it all came rushing back in her dreams. The Sun soothed and sang to her, and sparkling flowers passed in long lines, followed by a shadow called Forbidden.

Reena started getting up very early, before her parents were awake, and began roaming the silent passageways, searching for the oldest tapestries, the ones with the most flowers and plants, hoping they could somehow tell her more about Outside. Though she tried to hide it, her parents noticed a sadness in her eyes they had not seen before. "Dearest daughter, tell us what is wrong," they pleaded, but Reena knew she could not explain, for it might bring that lost look to their faces again.

One morning, Reena's searching brought her to a part of the cave she had not found before. She wasn't sure how she had gotten there or if she could ever find her way back, but on she went into the darkness, singing softly to herself for courage.

At each new turn, the trembling light of her candle revealed older and more detailed carvings along the walls. As Reena examined the petals of a lovely carved flower panel, she felt it move under her fingertips as if the bud itself had stirred to life. Cautiously she pushed again and the panel moved aside, revealing a narrow black crack. Thinking this opening might lead back to a familiar corridor, she squeezed through.

Reena found herself in a small mist-filled room that was like no other. There was a sharpness to the air that nipped at her nose and lips as she breathed. Then, suddenly, she caught her breath, for there in front of her hung the oldest tapestry she had ever seen.

In it was pictured a door that was open slightly, and on the other side could be seen green leaves and rays of brilliant light. Reena reached out to touch the aged threads. It was the gentlest touch, but to Reena's horror the weaving collapsed into a pile of dust at her feet. Her despair lasted but a moment, however, for there in front of her was the real door!

With only the slightest pause, she reached out a shaking hand, this time to a worn but solid handle.

Slowly, the handle turned with a terrible screech, and Reena pulled open the door. As a blast of bright light entered, pain like splinters shot through Reena's eyes. Crying out, she shielded her face and everything went black. At the same horrifying moment, she felt heat against her pale skin, as if she had walked too close to the hearth fire. Slowly the blackness faded, and in between her fingers seeped streaks of scarlet from an unknown light. Its presence comforted her, and inch by inch she lowered her hands . . . to the Sun!

There before her blazed the King of Red Sun Kings. His warmth filled her heart with a joy she had never felt before, as if she herself had been a carved wooden doll and was now miraculously brought to life. Reena wanted to stare into the Sun's face, but each time she tried, it burned her eyes. She realized that in her blindness, she had walked through the door. This must be Outside!

The protective cave ceiling no longer hovered over her head; now the sky, the real, never-ending sky, was above her and flowers were everywhere she looked, alive and sparkling in a prism of light. They swayed to the right, then to the left, set in motion by a cool gentle breeze that Reena could not see but could feel as it touched her warm forehead and tickled her cheek.

A path before her led into the valley, and she followed it, never wondering who made it or where it would lead. Lovingly she caressed all the growing things around her. It was not until the heat of the Sun began to burn her cave-white arms, that she suddenly remembered her parents and how worried they would be.

"I must go back and tell them of my wonderful discovery. Outside is real! It's not a dream."

Excitedly she turned—but wait! Something was wrong! The path had vanished, and she was surrounded by a tangle of flowers and vines. A feeling of weakness came over her.

"I think I had better sit down and rest for just a minute. Then I know I'll be able to find my way."

The ground was cool and Reena instantly fell into a deep sleep. A stillness spread over the valley as if all living things slept, even the breezes. All sleeping with Reena. Or waiting . . .

Then the mournsnap vines began to rustle, to slither and twist, and heavy footsteps broke the silence. Louder and louder. Closer and closer.

A dark shadow slid over Reena's small sleeping form and a grating laugh tore the air. A finger as rough as the end of a stick scraped against her still cheek. The laughter turned into a chanting song.

"At last, at last I have my beauty,
at last I have my life.
My power had faded along with my sight,
but now you've come to put it right.
Oh mournsnap vines in power mine,
hold for me this beauty entwined."

The vines near Reena's feet began to grow, twisting toward her, over her toes and around her ankles, then upward to encircle her wrists. She was a prisoner now, held fast.

"Awake, my beauty, awake, let me gaze upon your lovely face," the voice croaked.

Reena began to stir, and finally she opened her eyes. A creature of the most horrible proportions, with eyes full of evil, was glaring into her face. Gasping, Reena fell backwards and closed her eyes. What nightmare could this be?

"Please," she whispered, "let this be a dream. Let me be back in my safe wonderful cave."

"It's no dream, my dear. I am the Okira," the creature snarled. "I trapped your ancestors when I was young. Then they stopped coming out of their cave, but I waited. I knew someone would come out again someday, and *you* did and I've *got you!*"

Reena winced as hot breath hissed against her cheek.

"Hee, hee, now you'll never get away. Never get away . . . never get away . . ."

The vines began to murmur and the droning song grew fainter. Then all was silent.

Had the creature really gone? Trying her best to conquer her fear, Reena slowly opened her eyes.

Indeed, the Okira had disappeared. Remembering the lost path, Reena bolted up, only to be pulled back to the ground.

"What is this?" she cried. "How did I get so tangled in these vines?" She began to tug and twist, but the harder she pulled, the tighter they seemed to grow. The more she struggled, the harder it became for her to move at all. Her arms and legs ached, and sobs escaped her lips as welts appeared on her wrists and ankles. Finally, not knowing what else to do, she sat exhausted and stared at the delicate bonds.

"Oh pretty vines that hold me, won't you let me go home to my dear parents? I'm sure they are so worried."

As her tears fell into the tangle of vines, Reena felt the tiniest trembling sensation at her wrists, as if the little tentacles had heard her and were trying to unwind themselves. Silently she waited, and then the trembling stopped.

I believe they really did try, she thought. Then the Okira's words came back.

"You'll never get away."

"I *will* get away. I must. Why did I ever want to come Outside? Why?"

Then she looked up at the red Sun and remembered. "You are truly so magnificent. If you could only help me now."

At that moment, Reena heard a skittering sound very near her elbow.

"What was that?" she whispered.

Could it be the Okira returning?

Carefully she turned toward the sound, until there in front of her she saw a tiny house made all of vines, with little rugs at the doorway and miniature curtains at the windows. But the most amazing thing about it was the two little frightened creatures that peeked up at her from the darkened interior.

Their faces were so big-eyed and beaky and their bodies in such a tremble, Reena immediately felt sorry for them. "Don't be afraid, little dears. What has upset you?" she said in her most soothing voice.

Shyly they stepped into the light, and began to croak and squeak until finally an answer emerged.

"We—ah—we were afraid you were going to pull our house down with all your tearing at the vines."

"Oh, I'm sorry. You're so darling I would never hurt you."

Now they were the ones to be amazed. No one had ever called them darling before. Instantly they were all smiles and bows, brushing and smoothing their little vests.

They were so funny Reena had to laugh; still she did remember her own unpleasant situation.

"Can you help me untangle myself from these vines? My name is Reena and I *must* get home. I've just seen this horrible creature called the Okira."

At the Okira's name, the little ones froze and began to shake anew.

"No, no, we can't help you. We're—ah—er—well . . . afraid of the Okira," they sputtered. "She calls us ugly and kicks dirt at us whenever she sees us. She put a spell on the vines, with her evil magic. That's why they hold you. They would really like to let you go. But none of us can fight the Okira's magic. It is too strong, too strong," they repeated, nodding their heads. "But . . . we can take care of you and feed you," they announced, and they disappeared inside their cottage.

"Wait! Please come back."

With a flick, they were back, scampering up the vines and into Reena's hand with some scrumptious red berries, which Reena ate gladly, for she was hungry.

"Thank you very much. Now please tell me again about the Okira's magic. Surely there is a way it can be broken and I can go home."

"It can't be broken, Reena. You're too pretty! The Okira gets her power from things that are beautiful. You can't escape."

"Don't say that," she cried. "We must think of something!"

The little ones scratched their elbows and noses, which they did when they thought very hard. Then one of them shouted, "Maybe Nimar knows a way!"

"Who's Nimar?" asked Reena.

"The cleverest one in the valley. He's been trying to think of a way to stop the Okira for a long time. We'll go get him."

"Oh please do, but can't just one go and one stay? I hate to be left here alone."

"You won't be alone, Reena. We'll send our friends to look after you. And if we ride the kelkit, we'll get there twice as fast."

Reena hardly had time to say, "What's a kelkit?" before the little ones darted into the vines behind their house and emerged with a gentle-looking winged creature.

Soon they were mounted and prepared to leave. Up the kelkit jumped and they blew away on the next passing breeze.

"Good-bye," they shouted.

"Good-bye."

Minutes after seeing her little friends disappear into the distance, Reena was surrounded by a group of friendly chattering creatures who looked like larger versions of her two tiny friends. They brought cakes and pies, and some cushions for Reena to sit on and an umbrella to shade her from the Sun, and then they sat around her in a circle.

"You've all been so kind!" said Reena. "But please tell me about Nimar. Will he really help me?"

"We don't know, Reena. He was not able to help your ancestors. We all tried, but finally, we could not. We're so sorry."

Reena's eyes filled with tears, thinking of the dear old ones in the stories. So that was what had happened, why Outside was forbidden. They had been snared, then withered and died, perhaps on this very spot, by these same vines that held her. The thought brought such a stab of pain to her heart, she cried out. At that moment all her new friends turned their heads and looked away towards the mountains. Reena turned too and could not believe what she saw.

The Sun was leaving her and taking the light with him. Blackness was filling the sky.

"Where is he going? What is happening?" cried Reena. The black sky was much more frightening than the dark cave had ever been.

"It is the night now, Reena. The Sun will return in the morning."

"No, no, I can't bear it," she sobbed, hardly listening. The tears she had bravely held back finally broke free and poured down her cheeks. Then someone whispered, "Nimar."

Reena looked up to see a creature who might have seemed hideous except that his eyes were filled with kindness and the warmth of the vanished Sun. Suddenly Reena was no longer afraid.

"Nimar," she repeated. "Can you help me?"

"I'm not sure, Reena. I have heard the Okira has a Ruby Crystal hidden in her lair that adds strength to her evil magic. But as long as she is near, in the valley or in the woods, the pathway there is hidden from me."

"Then how will I be free?"

"If you are to be free, the answer must come from within you. Listen!"

"But how?" asked Reena.

"The best thing now is to sleep, and then perhaps an answer will come."

Nimar handed her a delicate glass filled with starlight liquid, which Reena drank. Then repeating softly to herself, "An answer will come . . ." she went to sleep.

As the Sun returned the next morning, Reena awoke to greet it. Her despair was gone. She had dreamed of a way to be free!

Quickly she asked her friends for the things that she would need: a piece of bark, a knife to carve with, and some paint.

Reena set to work, with the vines loosening their hold a bit to make her task easier. When she had finished, all drew near to see what she had made.

It was a mask! One more terrifying to look at than the Okira's face.

"Oh, Reena," her little friends shouted when she put it on. "The Okira surely won't want you if she thinks you look like that," they laughed.

I just hope she'll allow the vines to release me, thought Reena.

The mask was finished in the nick of time. A grayness fell across the face of the Sun and they knew the Okira was near. Her friends ran to their hiding places and Reena curled low to the ground, clutching the mask to her face.

Soon they heard the Okira's harsh laugh.

"Beauty, beauty, let me see my beauty."

Again Reena felt the Okira's hot breath. With the speed of the kelkit she spun around and roared a mighty roar, right into the Okira's face.

The Okira's scream was louder still.

"What have you done? Where is my beauty?" Each shriek was louder than the one before.

"Where did this ugliness come from? Where? Where?"

The Okira's green fists beat at the air.

"Where is sheeee?" she shouted still louder, and began to jump up and down.

"I've waited years to regain my power! Now it's gone, she's gone!"

The Okira's face began to turn purple. Then it started to swell. Her face and body swelled larger and larger with fury, and each jump took her a little higher than the one before, until she wasn't even touching the ground anymore. Soon she was floating above them, shouting her anger to the sky.

"Amazing," they whispered. "Incredible."

This had never happened before, not in the valley of the Boa-Bickle tree. Up into the crystal blue sky, the purple Okira floated until she was the tiniest speck.

The repentant vines uncurled their embrace and one by one they slithered away.

"It worked. She's free," her friends shouted.

"I'm free," whispered Reena.

Jubilation filled the valley as Reena and her friends started down the path towards her home.

"Wait, Reena!"

There was Nimar standing beside her.

"Nimar, come, we must hurry!"

"I cannot go with you. The task is not yet completed."

"What do you mean? We're free—the Okira is gone."

"I think she will soon return, Reena. She will realize she has been tricked. Now may be my only chance to go to her lair in the Tangled Forest and find the Ruby Crystal. I'm sure the path will be clear. Your strength would help me on this journey."

Much as Reena longed to return home, she knew Nimar was right. After all, he had helped her to dream of her escape.

"Yes, I'll come," Reena agreed.

"This will speed our journey." Behind them a large beast was being fastened to a cart. In they jumped and down into the valley they dashed. Sooner than Reena expected, they entered the gloom of the Tangled Forest, where only flickering glimpses of the Sun guided them along the newly opened path. No breeze could be felt here and no scent of flowers.

At last, they saw the Okira's den before them, caught in a snarl of decaying roots.

Nimar and Reena slipped from the cart and tiptoed to the door. What an amazing sight! In this place, where Reena expected to see only grotesque objects, she saw instead trucks filled with beautiful clothes, carved vases, and delicate jewelry.

"Nimar, look, it's wonderful."

As Reena started to rush forward to examine it all, Nimar clutched her shoulder.

"Reena," he whispered, "it all belonged to your ancestors trapped by the Okira."

Reena's face went pale. "Oh, Nimar." She turned and buried her face in his sleeve. "You knew this was here, didn't you?"

"Yes, I knew."

Together they heaped the precious objects into the cart, and then they began their frantic search for the Ruby Crystal.

"I've found it," shouted Nimar, emerging from a deep alcove, with a ruby ball sparkling in his hands.

"Quickly now, we must hurry."

Wrapping the glass tightly in a piece of cloth, they left the cavern.

Soon they were back in the sunshine of the valley, where their friends were waiting. Happily they all raced towards Reena's cave and her loving parents—but not unseen!

From her vantage point high in the sky, the Okira watched the gleeful procession, her eyes keener with distance than close up.

"I've been tricked," she growled, and then she began to laugh. "What a fine game! All the more fun because you tried to get away, silly girl!"

Flapping her arms very fast, she descended.

As fast as the beast could pull it, the cart full of adventurers rounded the last hill. There in the distance was the door, no longer forbidden but welcoming.

"Look, up above us," shouted a little one. Instantly they recognized the ominous shape coming towards them.

"Faster!" screamed Reena. "We must reach the door!"

"No you don't, my dear!"

The ground shook as the Okira landed in front of the door.

"No, no," cried Reena.

"Catch them, mournsnap vines!"

The vines around the door coiled to spring as Reena and her friends jumped from the cart.

"It won't work, Okira!" yelled Nimar. *"We have your crystal!"*

Reena held the ruby glass high, and then, with all her might, she threw it to the ground, where it broke into a hundred pieces.

"Fools!" snarled the Okira. "Did you think that glass was the source of my power? *No! My power is that I want you more than you want to be free!"*

"It's not true," cried Reena.

"Vines, get them!"

The vines flashed towards Nimar, whipped around his shoulders, then turned towards the girl.

"Stop!" screamed Reena, the sight of her dear Nimar entrapped giving her a newfound strength.

"Never, never will you trap me again and never will you hurt my friends. Nimar will be free!"

The vines wavered, and at that instant, Reena's parents, who had been searching for her, pulled open the forbidden door. Seeing them Reena shouted:

"And never will you trap my parents!"

The Okira, who had been pressed against the door, fell backwards into the cave.

"You'll die!" she screamed, struggling to recover herself. But Reena knew the Okira's power had been broken when the vines flew into the dark opening and spun themselves around her.

"She's lost her power!" Nimar shouted.

The friends seized the Okira and dragged her to the smallest, darkest, deepest room in the cave.

Now they were all free. Free to walk outside in the warmth of the Sun or rest inside the cool cave. No one felt the joy of this more than Reena, who was finally and truly free to explore with Nimar all the unexpected twists and turns of the Valley of the Bao-Bickle tree.

As for the Okira, there she sits to this day, knitting her ancient spells into the cave-spider's web lest she forget them. Many have visited her, for she too has an interesting story to tell. But if you should go there, be careful and remember—never, never unlock the door and let her out. It is forbidden.

*To all my dear friends who have walked beside me
on my journey. With special thanks to Barbara Hazan,
Jean Karl, Sandy Hardy, and my editor Regina Hayes
for their support and guidance.*

VIKING KESTREL
Published by the Penguin Group
Viking Penguin Inc., 40 West 23rd Street, New York, New York 10010, U.S.A.
Penguin Books Ltd, 27 Wrights Lane, London W8 5TZ England
Penguin Books Australia Ltd, Ringwood, Victoria, Australia
Penguin Books Canada Ltd, 2801 John Street, Markham, Ontario, Canada L3R 1B4
Penguin Books (N.Z.) Ltd, 182–190 Wairau Road, Auckland 10, New Zealand

Penguin Books Ltd, Registered Offices: Harmondsworth, Middlesex, England

First published in 1988 by Viking Penguin Inc.
Published simultaneously in Canada
Copyright © Marilee Heyer, 1988
All rights reserved
Library of Congress Cataloging in Publication Data
Heyer, Marilee.   The forbidden door/by Marilee Heyer.   p. cm.
Summary: Although her people have been forced to live underground
for many years by the evil Okira, Reena discovers the forbidden door
to the outside world and manages to free them.
ISBN 0-670-81740-6   [1. Fantasy.] I. Title. PZ7.H4498Fo 1988 [E]–dc 19   88-6072   CIP

Color separations by Imago Ltd., Hong Kong
Printed in Hong Kong by South China Printing Company
Set in Adroit Light.
1 2 3 4 5 92 91 90 89 88